In memory of my father, and for my sons whose early enthusiasm
for mazes and myths sowed the seeds of this book. – J.R.

For Charles – J.S.

JANETTA OTTER-BARRY BOOKS

Text copyright © Juliet Rix 2014
Illustrations copyright © Juliet Snape 2014
The rights of Juliet Rix and Juliet Snape to be identified respectively
as the author and illustrator of this work have been asserted by them in accordance
with the Copyright, Designs and Patents Act, 1988 (United Kingdom).

First published in Great Britain and in the USA in 2014 by
Frances Lincoln Children's Books,
74-77 White Lion Street, London N1 9PF
www.franceslincoln.com

A catalogue record for this book is available from the British Library.

ISBN 978-1-84780-431-0

Illustrated with watercolour
Set in Albertus MT

Printed in China

1 3 5 7 9 8 6 4 2

A-MAZE-ING MINOTAUR

Written by JULIET RIX

Illustrated by JULIET SNAPE

F

FRANCES LINCOLN
CHILDREN'S BOOKS

King Minos was a very powerful man – but he was not
a very nice one. At his luxurious palace on the beautiful island
of Crete, he kept a strange and dangerous beast. The Minotaur,
part man, part bull, lived in a vast maze of narrow corridors
and dark rooms – the Labyrinth. Once inside, no one could
find their way out, or so it was believed. Every nine years,
King Minos fed the Minotaur a terrible meal: fourteen young
people, seven boys and seven girls, brought across the water
from Athens. The Athenians didn't want to send their children
to die, but they didn't dare defy King Minos.

Theseus, Prince of Athens, was just the right age to be sent to Crete. To the horror of his father, the king, he insisted on going.

"I will kill the Minotaur," he declared.

Theseus and the other young Athenians set sail, and were greeted in Crete by King Minos himself.

"You have one night left to live," he said. "Feast and make merry. Tomorrow you go into the Labyrinth."

At the king's side was a beautiful girl. Theseus noticed her immediately – and she could not take her eyes off Theseus. Her name was Ariadne and she was King Minos's daughter.

Later that night, when the palace was quiet, Ariadne found Theseus alone. He was desperately trying to work out a plan. How could he kill the Minotaur with his bare hands? And how would he find his way out of the Labyrinth?

"I can help you," said Ariadne.

At first Theseus was suspicious. Ariadne was Minos's daughter, after all. But the princess had fallen in love with Theseus and she convinced him that she too feared her father's cruelty.

Ariadne gave Theseus a sword, small enough to hide in his tunic, and a ball of golden thread. "Unravel it as you go into the Labyrinth," she said, "and you will always be able to find your way out."
She promised to be at the door of the maze when Theseus returned.

Theseus fell asleep with the golden ball clutched to his heart.

The next day, with great fanfare, the young Athenians were taken to the Labyrinth. The Cretans watched, certain that these young people would never be seen again. The heavy doors to the maze swung open. Theseus and his friends were thrust inside and the doors clanged shut behind them.

It was dark in the Labyrinth and the youngsters shivered with fear. But Theseus went straight into action. He tied the golden thread to the Labyrinth door and told his friends, "You must wait here until I return." They protested that he should not go alone, but Theseus was resolute. "I am Prince of Athens," he said. "It is my job to get you safely away from here."

So Theseus set off into the Labyrinth, the golden ball in one hand, Ariadne's sword in the other.

He stepped slowly in the darkness, carefully unravelling the golden thread.

There were so many corridors, so many corners. Sometimes Theseus met a dead end, or went right round in a circle and nearly tripped over his own golden thread.

His heart was pounding, but he knew he had to be brave. He had the sword and the golden thread. His friends depended on him. Ariadne believed in him. He must end the terror of the Minotaur.

So on he went, unwinding the thread behind him, alert for any sound of the monster.

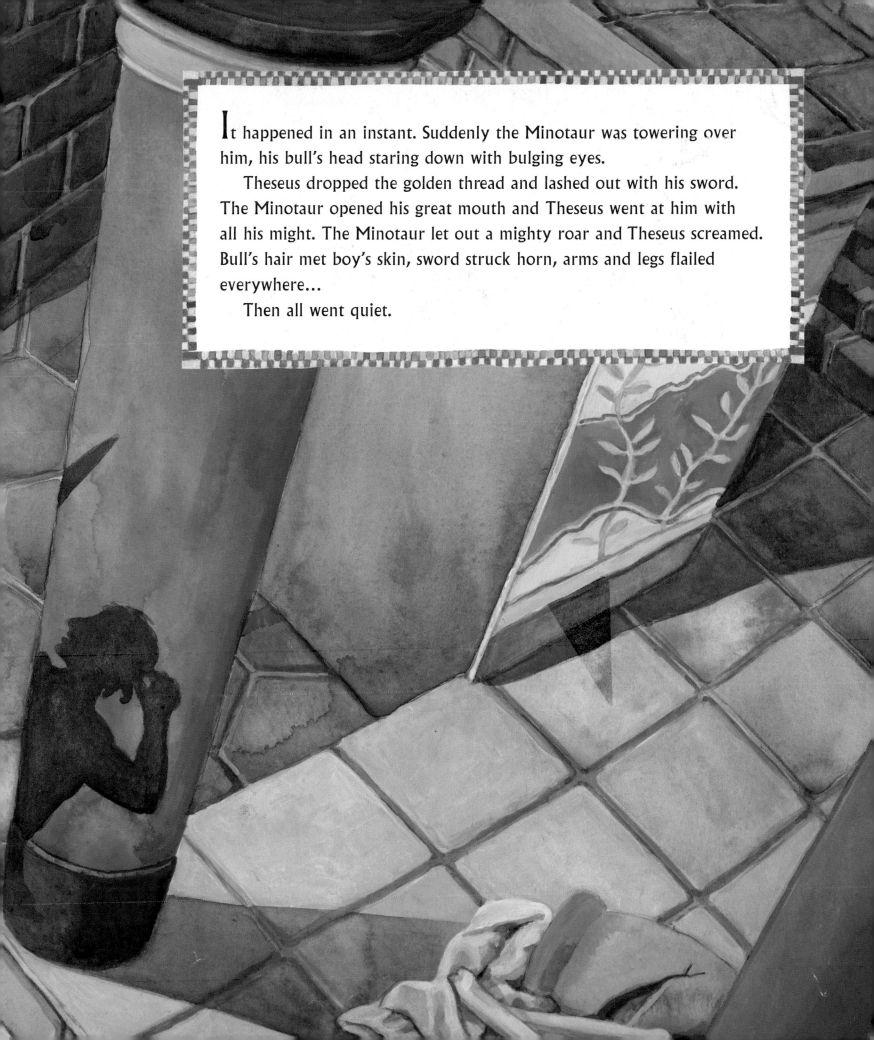

It happened in an instant. Suddenly the Minotaur was towering over him, his bull's head staring down with bulging eyes.

Theseus dropped the golden thread and lashed out with his sword. The Minotaur opened his great mouth and Theseus went at him with all his might. The Minotaur let out a mighty roar and Theseus screamed. Bull's hair met boy's skin, sword struck horn, arms and legs flailed everywhere...

Then all went quiet.

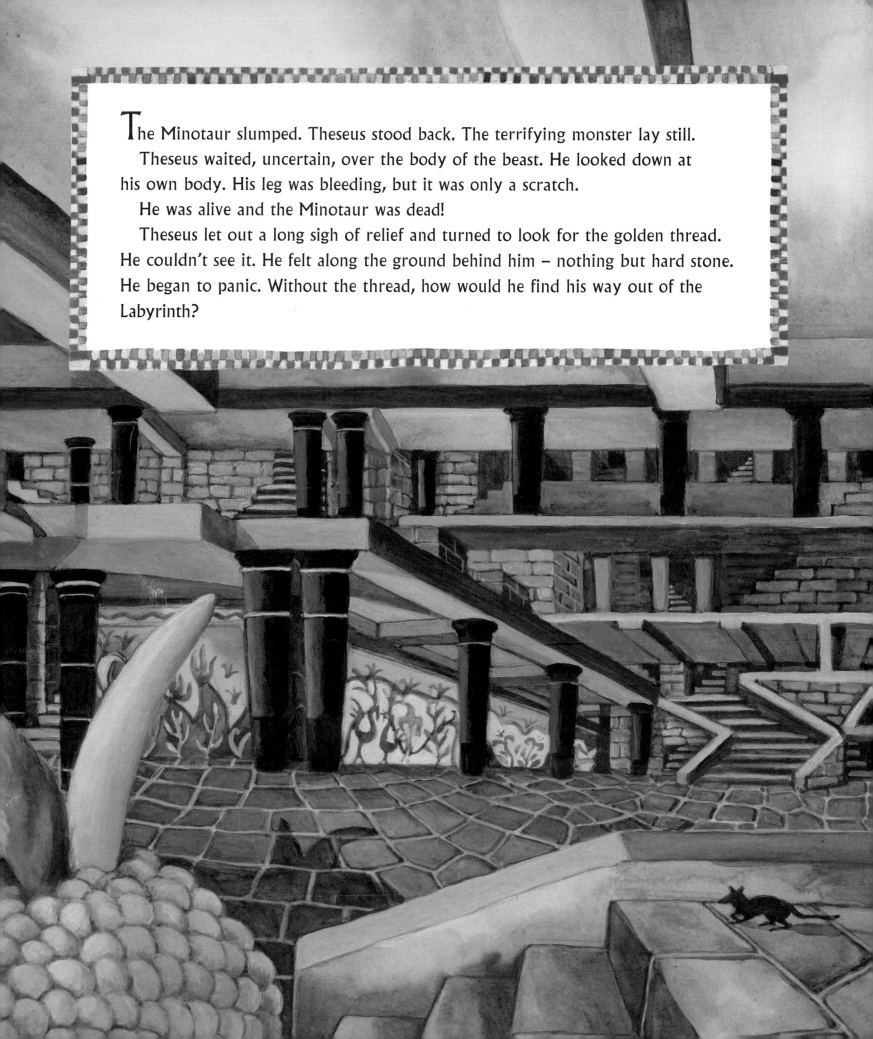

The Minotaur slumped. Theseus stood back. The terrifying monster lay still.

Theseus waited, uncertain, over the body of the beast. He looked down at his own body. His leg was bleeding, but it was only a scratch.

He was alive and the Minotaur was dead!

Theseus let out a long sigh of relief and turned to look for the golden thread. He couldn't see it. He felt along the ground behind him – nothing but hard stone. He began to panic. Without the thread, how would he find his way out of the Labyrinth?

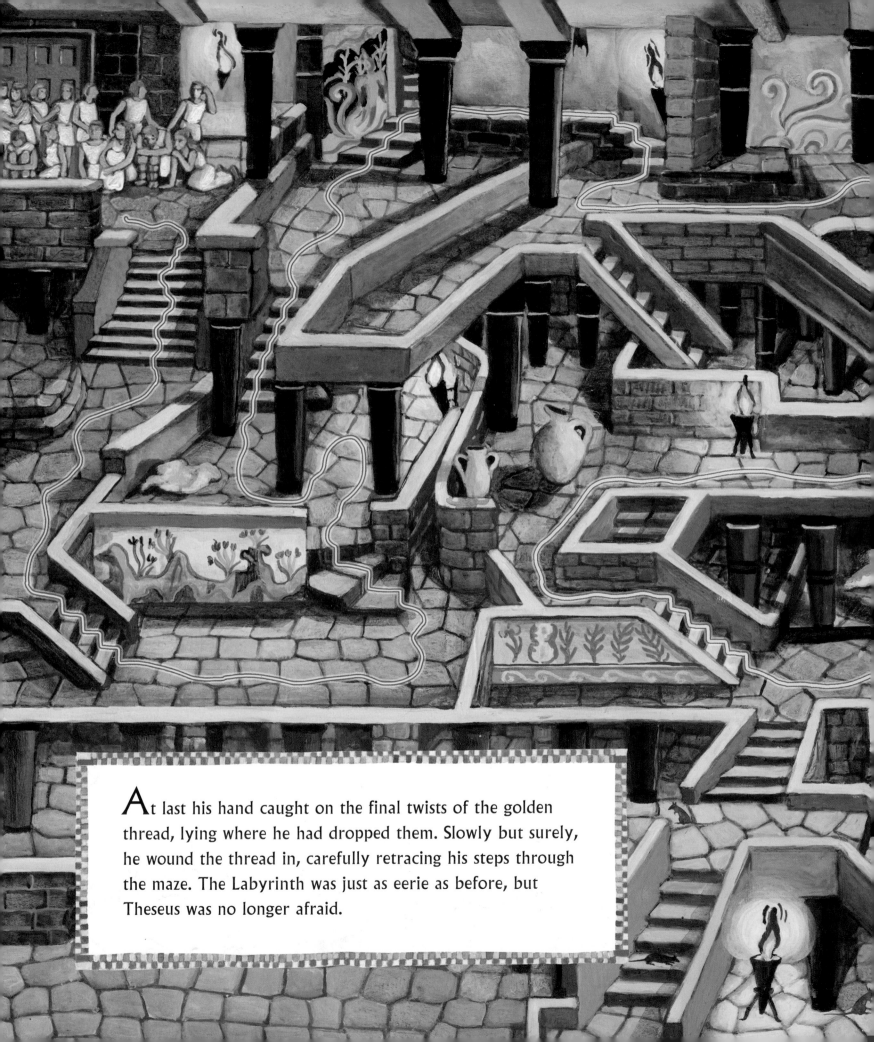

At last his hand caught on the final twists of the golden thread, lying where he had dropped them. Slowly but surely, he wound the thread in, carefully retracing his steps through the maze. The Labyrinth was just as eerie as before, but Theseus was no longer afraid.

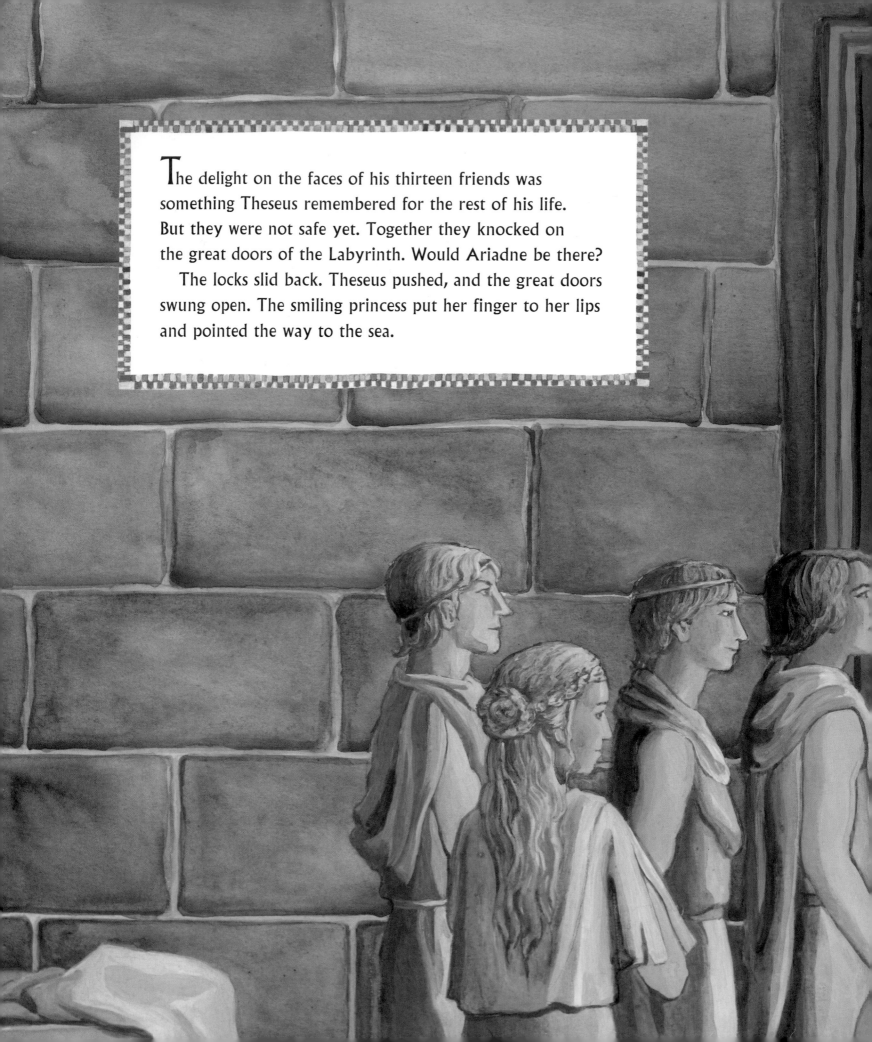

The delight on the faces of his thirteen friends was something Theseus remembered for the rest of his life. But they were not safe yet. Together they knocked on the great doors of the Labyrinth. Would Ariadne be there?

The locks slid back. Theseus pushed, and the great doors swung open. The smiling princess put her finger to her lips and pointed the way to the sea.

Quickly and quietly, Theseus and Ariadne and their Athenian friends ran to where their ship lay waiting. Swiftly they boarded, silently they loosed the ropes and the ship moved soundlessly away.

Not a word passed their lips, but they could see the joy in each other's eyes as Theseus and Ariadne embraced. Never again would King Minos take the lives of young Athenians to feed his monstrous Minotaur.

The truth behind the story

Crete is one of the Greek islands, and on the outskirts of the modern capital, Heraklion, you can visit the remains of Knossos, the centre of Minoan civilisation. The buildings here were excavated by the British archaeologist Sir Arthur Evans, who believed them to be the remains of the Palace of Minos.

The story of the Minotaur is a myth, but the Minoans were real enough and they ruled Crete for 1500 years, from around 5000 years ago. They built great palaces and towns across the island, the remains of which can still be seen today.

No Labyrinth has been found at Knossos, but excavations have revealed a vast complex of buildings with a large central courtyard reached by an angled corridor and surrounded by over 1000 interconnecting rooms. Could the palace itself have been 'the Labyrinth'?

Archaeologists have also uncovered fragments of Minoan paintings on the walls at Knossos (the originals are now in the Heraklion Museum) and at other Minoan sites on Crete. The pictures in this book were inspired by the Minoan style of art and architecture.

GREECE

TURKEY

Athens

Knossos

CRETE